ENZO
RACES IN THE RAIN!

Garth Stein
with Zoë B. Alley and R. W. Alley

Illustrated by R. W. Alley

HARPER
An Imprint of HarperCollinsPublishers

Text copyright © 2014 by Garth Stein
Additional text credit: Zoë B. Alley and R. W. Alley
Illustrations copyright © 2014 by R. W. Alley

Library of Congress Control Number: 2014931072
ISBN 978-0-06-293966-1

The artist used pen and ink, pencil, watercolor, gouache, acrylics,
and coffee spills on paper to create the illustrations for this book.
Typography by Rachel Zegar
19 20 21 22 23   PC   10 9 8 7 6 5 4 3 2 1

❖

First Edition

For Comet,
always a puppy at heart
—G.S.

To Minni, who has informed
our writing and drawing!
—Z.B.A. and R.W.A.

From the start, I've known that I was different.

On the outside, I'm the same as all the other new pups on the farm. But on the inside—in my head, in my heart—that's not who I am.

I feel more like a person. When people talk, I want to join in. I want them to listen and say, "Yes, yes, we know exactly what you mean." But they don't understand my barks.

It drives me crazy.

What makes me happy is to run as fast
as I can through the sweet-smelling fields.
I tear along the fence by the big road.

I race the cars that pass the farm.
They smell of gasoline and rubber.

I bark to the people inside,
"Where are you going?"
Of course, they don't understand.

I think I drive the old farmer crazy, too.
After all these weeks, he's never named me.
"Stop your barking, dog," he snaps.
That's all I get. "Dog."

One day, I see a cloud of dust blowing down the barn road toward us.

It's a car running like I've never heard before. Not chugging like the old man's tractor but smooth and even, the way I feel when I run.

I race to meet it. But it is fast. Really fast.

A girl in the car is waving at me.

The girl and a big man get out. I see that the girl is small—a puppy like me.

The car smells like the others, but there is a new smell, too. It is sweet and clean. It is the little girl.

The next moment, the girl has her arms around me.
I try to squirm away, then stop. I do like that smell.
And her hug makes me feel happy.

"Daddy, this is the one!" she says.

"Well, Zoë, he sure can run," says her dad.

"He's like a race car driver without a car," says Zoë.

"Has he got a name?" Zoë's dad asks.

"Naw. Hasn't stayed in one place long enough to get one," says the old man. "He's always runnin'!"

Zoë's dad smiles. "Well, that makes him just about perfect for us."

All at once the old man has me by the scruff of
the neck. He puts me in a cardboard box.

"Wait," says Zoë. She places a small pile of hay
under me. I snuggle down into it.

Then the old man folds the box flaps shut.

It is darker than the barn at night.

Click, click.

Vroom.

Suddenly, I'm moving!
I can't believe it! I'm in the car!

I push the box flaps open.
The car is going fast, faster than
I've ever run.

I watch out the window as the
world speeds by.
Nothing can catch us.

I can't help myself.
I bark in delight.

"I knew you were a racer," says Zoë. She scruffles
me behind the ears and it feels good.

"Daddy, I bet if he could drive, he'd be a race car
driver, just like you."

Racing means going fast. Yes, yes, I could be a race
car driver!

"Then he'll need a race car driver's name," says Zoë's dad.

"And you've already taken Denny Swift," laughs Zoë.

"Why don't we name him after Enzo Ferrari?" says Denny. "He's one of the greatest racers ever. When he was racing, he never gave up."

"Just Enzo," says Zoë.

Enzo, one of the greatest racers ever! That's me!

I bark twice.

Denny chuckles. "What's that, Enzo? Does two barks mean faster?"

The trees get taller. Everything gets greener.
Who knew the world was so big?

Finally we slow down. We're on a street with
lots of small houses and cars that aren't moving.
"Here we are," says Denny.
"Home, Enzo," says Zoë.
This feels good. I'm so happy, I want to run!
But then Denny carries me inside.

Inside smells are new.
There's nowhere to run inside.

"Come on, Enzo, take a look at your new house!" Zoë says. "Here's my room."

What's on her bed? They look like animals, but they don't move.

They just stare at me.

I don't like being stared at.

I growl at them.

"You can sleep here, beside me
and my stuffed animals," says Zoë.

Sleep? Not with those animals
staring at me.

I really want to run.

"Let's not forget to show Enzo the kitchen,"
says Denny. "Who's hungry?"

Yes, yes! I realize I am hungry. Very hungry.

"Let's have pancakes," says Zoë.

"Breakfast for dinner? Great idea," says Denny.
"Pancakes for all!"

"Look, Enzo," says Zoë. "Here's a racer's collar
so you won't get lost. And a special in-and-out door
just for you!"

When she pushes the door flap, I smell grass
and trees and outside.

Before Zoë can snap on the collar,
I leap through the door. I am outside!
But it is a very small outside.

I start to run, but a fence and bushes stop me.

Then I spy a gap under the fence.

There's always a field beyond a fence, isn't there?

I squeeze through.

I tumble onto hard pavement.
Cars are going everywhere.
Finally, I can run!

I run with one car.
Then another. And another.
Pretty soon, there are too
many cars.

HONK! HONK!

"Get out of the road, you
crazy dog!"

Now people are running everywhere—
all sprinting after me!
They like to run, too! This is fun!

Suddenly, the sky darkens.
FLASH! CRACK!
Rain comes down. The people run away.
It's a cold, hard rain. So cold, it hurts my nose.
So hard, it stings the pads on my paws.
I try to find a place that's warm and dry.

This isn't fun anymore!
    I miss Denny and Zoë—their smells
and warm hugs.
    I want to go home!
    But where *is* home?

Wait! I remember I am named Enzo—
after the race car driver who never gave up!
I run like a racer through the rain!
I stop, sniff, run.

Where was that gap in the fence?
Pancakes! I smell Denny's pancakes!
I smell Zoë.
There's the gap! I scramble under
the fence.

I burst through my Enzo door.
Look, I made it!

I race into Zoë's room. But my wet
paws skid, and I slide against Zoë's bed.
Her animals fall all over me! Oh no!
Wait—they smell like Zoë. Sweet and
clean and fresh and good.
I wish Zoë and Denny were here.

Then, from the other room, I hear *click* and *squeak* and footsteps.

Zoë is crying. "He's gone, Daddy," she says. "He'll never come back."

"Honey, it's not your fault," says Denny. "He's smart like a race car driver. He won't give up. Enzo will find his way home."

Enzo? Hey, that's me! I bark twice.

I run into Zoë's arms like a race car driver speeding home. "Enzo, you're here!" Zoë exclaims. They are hugging me and rubbing my cold, wet fur. It feels so good to be home.

That's when I hear it—it is Denny saying to me, "Yes, yes, I know exactly what you mean. It is good to be home!"